I0785613

VAEDRA CHRONICLES COMPANION II

A VISUAL LOOK AT THE VAEDRA SYSTEM

THE GENESIS AND THE VAEDRA SAGAS

ESTER LÓPEZ

Illustrated by
NANOAOI

Illustrated by
ESTER LÓPEZ

Writing & Photographic Services LLC

All characters in this book are fictitious and any resemblance to actual persons living or dead, places, events, or locales is purely coincidental.

All rights reserved.

No part of this book may be reproduced in any form or by any electronic or mechanical means, including information storage and retrieval systems, without written permission from the author, except for the use of brief quotations in a book review.
This book may contain mature content and is intended for adult readers
Cover Design Copyright © 2023
by Ester López
Illustrated by Nanoaoi
and
Ester López
ISBN PRINT: 979-8-9884483-2-7
ISBN ebook: 979-8-9884483-3-4

www.esterlopez.com

www.authorblogspot.esterlopez.com

www.facebook.com/EsterLopezAuthor

CONTENTS

ESTER'S READERS GROUP

Sign up for my Readers Group and get the first three chapters of the first three books in the Genesis Saga of the Vaedra Chronicles series, FREE!

Sign Up

ABOUT THE AUTHOR

Ester López is a writer and publisher and lives in the Smoky Mountains of Tennessee along with her husband, Jerry, and two miniature horses, Pepper & Bucky. She has been writing sci fi and paranormal adventure romances for almost 30 years. She also writes children's books.

In her spare time, Ester enjoys photography, sewing, arts and crafts, canning, gardening, and making her own wine.

To keep up to date on Ester's book releases, and to get the FREE "Vaedra Chronicles" companion book, please join Ester's Readers Group at:

www.esterlopez.com
Follow Ester's Blogs at:
www.esterlopez.com
www.authorblogspot.esterlopez.com
Follow Ester on:
www.facebook.com/EsterLopezAuthor
or on Twitter at:
www.twitter.com/esterlopez1

You can also join Ester's Group Page on Facebook at Virtual
Book Signing & Takeover Group

INTRODUCTION

Vaedra

The Vaedra Chronicles is a series of stories set in the Vaedra System and on Earth. The first part of the series is The Genesis Saga, which is now complete. The second part is the Vaedra Saga, which encompasses the planets in the Vaedra system.

Over a 1,000 anos (years) ago, in the Vaedran cycle, the

planet Vestra had become over-populated. The Council of Nations decreed to keep the races separated. They sent an exploratory mission to discover what planets, if any, were able to sustain life.

Throughout the Vaedra System, it was determined that many of the planets were habitable, as well as their moons. Colonies were planned to keep the races separate where they could rule themselves on their own planets.

Meanwhile, scientists worked feverishly on developing alternate methods of supplying power, fuel, and food sources for Vestra, as well as the new colonies being planned.

Colonization began on Persus, where it was as large as Vestra, but with six moons. There was plenty of room to accommodate the three tribes of Naronn descendants. The six moons are Hestia, Cyra, Pari, Asha, Val and Karush.

Next was Tarsius with its five moons, Mot, Lun, Veg, Ti and Hapnor. On this planet, the Junali descendants were sent to colonize the place and eventually separated into five major groups, according to their tribal councils. At the time of their migration, two moons had not been explored--Ti and Hapnor.

The remaining planets were Semtron, Vestra Minor, Plumaris, Atria, Chroma, and Plexus. Semtron was deemed uninhabitable due to its extremes in temperatures, as well as it being the closest to Vaedra, the sun.

Vestra Minor was inhabited by tribes descended from the Taecl'ann. Vestra Minor had no moons and the Taecl'ann people were small in number.

Atria became inhabited by tribes of Micca Nulee descent, with each tribe inhabiting different regions of the planet. Atria had one moon, Adara, which was deemed habitable.

Migration to Chroma with its six moons began later. Only one moon, Creton, had been explored at the time of migration. Chroma was colonized by those of Scandin descent. The most savage of these descendants lived on Creton.

The migration to Plexus by the descendants of the Huanti people began last. At that time, all three moons, Nela, Tiga, and Meta had been explored and deemed habitable. However, the tribes of the Huanti were small enough that the moons were not needed. Only one moon, Meta, had secretly been inhabited.

Plumaris had a vast source of tulin, titanium, and helium gases. The three moons, Ata, Beya, and Dena, held other sources of ore, precious metals, crystals, as well as some undiscovered ores. The Council of Nations would decide the fate of this planet and its moons at a later date. In the meantime, it would be used as a penal colony.

Leviticus Station, known as the "Gates of Hell" was established there to hold criminals convicted of violent crimes. They served their time mining these ores, gases, and metals. The heavily guarded Station was self-sufficient due to the kashis (money) being made from the mined ores and metals. Some of the profits of these metals went to the families of the victims or persons the crime was committed against until restitution was made.

Vestra became Vestra Major when Vestra Minor was colonized. The tribes remaining on Vestra Major were all descended from the Caucus people, whose numbers were as great as the Naronn. Vestra Major's one moon, is uninhabitable.

ISP Space Station (Deposit Photo)

The Interplanetary Space Patrol

Over 100 anos ago, in the Vaedran cycle, the Interplanetary Space Patrol (I.S.P.) was formed to enforce safe space travel between the planets and outer rim. They enforced the laws set by the Council of Nations. Four main space stations, where travelers could re-fuel both their ships and bodies, as well as short term stay-overs, are strategically located throughout the system. Several smaller stations, independently run for profit, were sprinkled between the planets and moons. The "Indie Stations" were regulated by the council to assure all trade was fair among the stations.

Vestra Major's Sentinel City (Deposit Photo)

Government

Each planet governs itself with tribal councils deciding among them the best course of action to deal with their own laws and problems. Each tribe has at least two representatives that go to the tribal council meetings each moon cycle. Then, when the Council of Nations meets twice an ano, the tribal council sends two representatives from each tribe to report on the progress of each colony.

Each tribe contributes to the cost of the governing body's

expenses for travel. All representatives are volunteers and are not paid for their time.

The official language of all planets is Vaedran dialect, but each planet may choose one or more languages to be used on their planet.

Plumaris as seen from Beya, one of it's moons (Deposit Photo)

DICTIONARY OF VAEDRAN TERMS

- Baroo - bear-like creature
- Capu - a form of coffee
- Cleansing Unit - shower/toilet/sink
- Cleansing Compartment or CleansCom - bathroom
- Command Room - controls incoming/outgoing spacecraft as well as communications within building/compound (like a dispatcher/FAA type person)
- Comm-Link - communications device worn or carried on person
- COMM pad - a communication device (similar to clipboard/iPad) that can bring up information or be written onto with a stylus. A type of computer-like data pad, portable and lightweight.
- Dinnaras - dollars
- Eating Hall - dining room/cafeteria
- Eating Implement - a fork-like spoon
- Fissal - napkin

- Hand Restraints - type of handcuff
- HPM - horizontal people mover moving people from one plane to another horizontally at a high rate of speed
- Hover-Trol - a hovering dolly to move heavy objects
- Inebrium - a sweet liquid similar to wine
- Illuminator - a light source
- Intercom-link - communications within a ship from quarters to quarters
- Kashis – money
- Keypad - similar to keyboard but smaller
- Kiks - 1 kilometer
- Kunnarled - screwed, messed up
- Light Stick - similar to flashlight
- Malloid - a composite of various metals
- Miniate - a small person or dwarf
- Nav-room - Navigation room on a spacecraft/cockpit
- Nav-U-Com - Navigational Unit Computer used to fly spacecraft and navigate space
- Nelu Berry - dewberry
- Quastic - tent-like fashion
- Shiv - a sack-like outfit used to clothe the slaves (similar to pillow case with holes for head and arms) short in length, barely covering thighs
- Skunt - slang term for low-life
- Stickit - game similar to pool, played on a round table using a stickit (pool stick) and 4 different colored sets of balls and one black ball
- Trew - beef stew
- Tulin - gold, higher quality on the Vaedra System
- Unicrin - uniform

- VPM - Vertical People Mover that moves people from one location to another on a vertical plane at a high rate of speed.
- Yav - a card-like device used to open doors, cages, anything with a lock
- Yetik – plastic

The Guardian (On loan to Genesis from the ISP)

1

DELETED SCENES FROM THE ABDUCTION

These scenes were done by the artist, Nanoaoi. She did an excellent job depicting what was in my head with little description. I hope you enjoy them.

VAEDRA, THE NAME BY WHICH WE CALL OUR SUN. THE CENTER OF AN ELLIPTICAL GALAXY, VAEDRA SHEDS HER LIGHT ON NINE PLANETS AND THEIR MOONS.
THE FIRST PLANET IN THE VAEDRA SYSTEM, VESTRA, WAS TEAMING WITH LIFE.
THE COUNCIL OF NATIONS DECIDED THAT TO SUSTAIN LIFE AND KEEP THE RACES PURE, AN EXPLORATORY MISSION WOULD SET OUT TO DISCOVER
WHAT PLANETS, IF ANY, WERE HABITABLE. DECADES LATER, EIGHT OF VAEDRA'S NINE PLANETS WERE COLONIZED. VESTRA IS HOME TO THE CAUCUS PEOPLE.
PERSUS, A PLANET AS LARGE AS VESTRA MAJOR BUT WITH SIX MOONS. IT ACCOMMODATES THE THREE TRIBES OF NARONN DESCENDANTS. THE SIX MOONS ARE HABITABLE BUT NOT COLONIZED AT THIS TIME. THEY ARE HESTIA, CYRA, PARI, ASHA, VAL, AND KURUSH.
THE JUNALI DESCENDANTS LIVE ON TARSIUS IN FIVE MAJOR GROUPS. THE MOONS, MOT, LUN, AND VEG ARE HABITABLE BUT NOT COLONIZED. TI AND HAPNOR HAVE NOT BEEN EXPLORED AS YET.
SEMTRON WAS DEEMED UNINHABITABLE DUE TO ITS EXTREME TEMPERATURES AS WELL AS ITS CLOSENESS TO VAEDRA.
VESTRA MINOR, SMALLER THAN VESTRA MAJOR, WAS INHABITED BY TRIBES DESCENDED FROM THE TAECLE'ANN, WHICH WAS SMALL IN NUMBER.

ATRIA WAS INHABITED BY TRIBES OF MY PEOPLE, THE MICCA NILEE, WITH EACH TRIBE INHABITING DIFFERENT REGIONS OF THE PLANET. MY NAME IS GENESIS AND MY TRIBE IS FROM WHITE MOUNTAIN BUT MY STORY WILL COME LATER. OUR ONLY MOON, ADARA IS HABITABLE BUT CURRENTLY UNPOPULATED.
CHROMA'S PEOPLE LIVE IN CLANS AND ARE OF SCANDIN DESCENT. ONLY ONE MOON, CRETON, HAD BEEN EXPLORED AND THE MOST SAVAGE OF THESE CLANS LIVE ON CRETON.
PLEXUS ACCOMMODATES THE HUANTI DESCENDANTS. IT'S THREE MOONS, NELA, TIGA, AND META ARE ALL HABITABLE BUT NONE ARE POPULATED AT THIS TIME, EXCEPT META, WHICH IS THE HOME BASE TO DRAM, THE SLAVE-TRADER.
THE INTERPLANETARY SPACE PATROL WAS UNAWARE THAT DRAM'S BASE WAS LOCATED ON THE MOON, META, OF THE PLANET, PLEXUS. HE OPERATED THERE FOR 25 AÑOS (YEARS) UNDETECTED.
PLUMARIS IS HABITABLE, BUT MANY OF THE METALS THAT ARE MINED THERE CAN CAUSE DAMAGE TO THE BODY WITH PROLONGED EXPOSURE SO IT'S MOSTLY USED AS A PENAL COLONY. THE THREE MOONS ARE ATA, BEYA, AND DENA.
HUNTER FOR THE I.S.P. OR THE INTERPLANETARY SPACE PATROL UNTIL ONE FATEFUL DAY, I MADE THE MISTAKE OF CAPTURING THE WRONG MAN.

DELETED SCENE FROM "THE ABDUCTION" ATRIA WHILE THE MEN AND YOUNG BOYS HUNTED BAROO, THE WOMEN AND CHILDREN PICKED MAIZE. THE OLD ONES WATCHED AFTER THE BABIES.
WHY DON'T YOU AND THE GIRLS HAVE A RACE TO SEE WHO CAN FILL THEIR BASKETS AND TAKE THEM TO THE OLD ONES BEFORE ANYONE ELSE?
WOULD THAT BE FAIR? I AM THE FASTEST IN THE TRIBE.
YOU MAY BE THE FASTEST RUNNER, GENESIS, BUT LET'S SEE WHO CAN GATHER THEIR MAIZE AND FILL THE BASKETS THE FASTEST.
YOU MUST COMPLETE A FULL ROW TO WIN A PRIZE, A BEAUTIFUL BRACELET, HAND-MADE BY ME.
READY, SET, GO!
GOOD JOB!

THAT WAS THE LAST TIME I SAW MY FATHER'S MOTHER.
GENESIS HEARS SCREAMING BABIES, GIRLS AND MOTHERS
AAAAHH!!
AAAAH!!
NOO!!
NO!
RUN GENESIS! GET YOUR FATHER!
FORGET HER, DRAM, LET'S GO!

MALEK! HELP!
MALEK! HELP!
WHAT IS IT, GENESIS? WHAT'S WRONG?
ALL THE WOMEN AND YOUNG ONES ARE BEING ATTACKED!
YIP, YIP, YIP, HAW!
THE WOMEN ARE BEING ATTACKED!

YOU MUST GO AFTER THEM.
WILL YOU KEEP WATCH OVER THE TRIBE WHILE I'M GONE?
OF COURSE
I'M GOING WITH YOU.
NO, GENESIS. YOU WILL STAY HERE WITH MALACHI.
YOU WANT ME, THE ONLY WOMAN AND YOUR ONLY CHILD, TO STAY HERE WITH ALL THESE MEN AND BOYS?
SHE HAS A POINT, MALEK. YOU DON'T KNOW HOW LONG THIS WILL TAKE.

ALL RIGHT, YOU CAN GO. WE WILL TAKE JOLU WITH US TO THE CAPITAL. HE CAN RETURN WITH THE CRUISER.
THAT WAS THE LAST TIME I SAW MY FATHER'S FATHER AND MY VILLAGE, TEN AÑOS AGO, WHEN I WAS FOURTEEN.
DELETED SCENE FROM "THE ABDUCTION"   EARTH
SHE'S ACTING MORE POSSESSIVE THE LONGER I'M AROUND HER.
SO, SHE LIKES YOU. IS THAT BAD?
SHE'S SMOTHERING ME. I LIKE BEING SINGLE. I CAN DO WHAT I PLEASE, WHEN I PLEASE.
SO TELL HER.
THAT'S NOT AN EASY TASK.

SURE IT IS.
I'VE GOT ANOTHER PROBLEM.
A STRAY CAT HAS TAKEN UP RESIDENCE AT MY CABIN AND IT NEEDS A GOOD HOME.
WHAT'S THAT?
YOU AND MISSY HAVE A COUPLE OF KIDS. YOU NEED A CAT.
SO WHAT'S THE PROBLEM?
NO, WE DON'T. YOU'RE THE ONE WHO NEEDS SOMETHING.
I'M FINE, REALLY. I DON'T NEED A WOMAN IN MY LIFE AND I CERTAINLY DON'T NEED A CAT.
THEY'RE BOTH TOO DEMANDING FOR MY TASTES.
ARE WE STILL ON FOR FISHING TOMORROW?
SURE. WHEN YOU STOP BY THE CABIN, YOU CAN CHECK OUT THE CAT. MISSY WILL LOVE IT.

LOOKS LIKE A STORM BREWING TONIGHT.
YEAH, I WANT TO GET HOME BEFORE IT HITS.
YOU FINISH THAT CABIN FOR JEREMY?
I FINISHED IT TODAY. THAT REMINDS ME... I NEED TO CELEBRATE.
LOOKS LIKE YOU GOT A NEW ADDITION TO YOUR FAMILY.
WHAT? OH, I DON'T HAVE A FAMILY. IT'S JUST A STRAY CAT. I'M GETTING JEREMY TO TAKE IT. HE'S GOT A FAMILY AND A GOOD HOME.
HOME IS WHERE THE HEART IS, YOU KNOW. SOME PEOPLE THINK THEIR PET IS THEIR FAMILY.
NOT ME.
BRRR!!

MEOW
DAMN CAT!
DON'T GET USED TO THIS, CAT. I FOUND YOU A GOOD HOME.

2

———

EXCERPT FROM THE ABDUCTION

Excerpt from The Abduction

Adrenalin pumped through his veins. His fisted hands were ready to fight. He stared into eyes the same pale blue as his and faced a man identical to himself, his brows narrowed in anger. He wrestled him to the ground. The other man's strength was a match for his own. When he shoved him down, the man reached for a strange-looking gun and took aim. He awoke the moment the man pulled the trigger.

Adam Davis bolted upright in his bed. His heart pounded from labored breathing. His body, moist with sweat, was still pumped and ready to fight but he was alone. He glanced around his dark cabin.

The sheet and thin bedspread fell away exposing his bare arms and chest. Rubbing the sleep from his eyes didn't eliminate the lingering dream. It was more like a premonition, like the one he'd had years ago that foretold the death of his parents.

Thunder growled outside. His pulse raced as other images came to mind. The first was a light bright as the sun. The second was a beautiful, dark-skinned young woman with high cheekbones and dressed in a white glowing jump-suit. She spoke to him, but he didn't understand the words.

Lightning flashed and a rumbling boom shook the tiny log cabin nestled in the foothills of the Smoky Mountains.

Thunderstorms were rare here but on a stormy night like this, his parents had died sixteen long years ago, when he was ten. The memory still tugged at his heart. Storms made him restless.

Another flash drew his attention to the picture window centered in the room which overlooked the pond.

Crack! The dwelling shook again. Two lights shone over the water, then moved toward the wooded area surrounding his home.

A plane? He threw off his bedding and approached the glass.

The soft glowing orbs sat low in the sky. Aircraft didn't fly below tree level did they? He ran a hand through his hair as he watched the flight path.

Suddenly, lightning struck one of the objects, brightening the entire sky. The explosion startled him. The cabin shook so hard the bed moved a few inches across the wood floor and the glass panes rattled.

"Oh my God!" Remembering the vision, he watched in horror as the fireball fell from the sky.

He yanked his clothes off the chair and pulled on his jeans. Hopefully someone would survive the crash. He slipped a sweatshirt on then struggled with his wading boots.

His raincoat hung by the door. Grabbing the yellow garment from the hook, he knocked his fishing poles on the floor.

"Damn!" Pulling the slicker on, he fastened the top two snaps. He considered the coiled rope on the chair for stabilizing broken bones then slipped it across his chest. Wood for splints was plentiful outside.

He hesitated at the door and lifted the bow and quiver of arrows off another peg. The black bear he had seen the other day might return for the berries beside the pond. His old Boy Scout motto, "be prepared" crossed his mind so he grabbed a flashlight.

The covered porch protected him from the rain but he left the warmth of his dry cabin to search for survivors.

The approaching daylight accompanied a heavy, cold rain, usual for August in the mountains. His boots stuck in the east Tennessee clay-like mud as he rushed through the woods. Each step got heavier as his waders gathered more muck. Icy droplets stung his face like sharp pellets. Breathing the moldy air, he quickly followed the worn path around the reedy pond. A glimmer of light shone in the distance.

God, he hoped no one had died. Memories of his parents' death came to mind--'Burned beyond recognition'-- a shiver ran down his spine. He quickened his pace, an uneasiness pulling at his gut. He hoped he wasn't too late. If someone had been there to help his parents, maybe they would be alive today.

Early daylight coupled with lightning, enabled him to find his way through the thickly wooded area. The secluded location of his home allowed him his privacy. He often thought of it as a blessing, since the place had once belonged to his grandparents. Injuries, though, would be a curse. Cell phones didn't work here in the mountains and the downpour would have washed most of the gravel away again. There was no way to get emergency help out here.

He arrived at the wreckage. The rain had almost put out the fire. The burned-out, smoldering shell that remained vaguely resembled a mangled football. Did anyone survive? Anxiety flowed over him as eerie shadows played around the object in the predawn light.

His gut told him to get out of there. He glanced up. No parachute. Maybe the pilot had bailed before the aircraft hit the ground. He blinked, wiping the drizzle from his face.

There were no signs of life. He walked toward the small plane. Another flash of lightning lit up the mangled mass.

Silently, he counted...one thousand one, one thousand two, one thousand three, one thou--

Boom! The storm moved farther away and the rain let up.

"Hey, is anybody here?" he shouted above the rumbling. No response. Closing the distance, he tried again. "Can you hear me?" Apprehension crept up the back of his neck, like someone watched him.

He pulled the bow off his shoulder, nocked an arrow to the bowstring and swung around to check the woods behind him. His bow, fully drawn was ready to release but aimed at nothing.

Lowering his draw, he blinked the rain from his eyes. He couldn't shake the feeling someone was out there. Facing the small plane, he walked toward it as another bolt lit up the area, brighter than before.

He gasped and his heart thudded. The flattened football-shaped object had no wings or tail. It was unlike anything he had ever seen. His first thought was to run like hell! But somebody might be alive in there. He shoved his arrow back in the quiver, and glanced over the area. He slung his bow on his shoulder and cracked his knuckles as he circled the heap of metal. The search for a way to get into the craft was futile.

He needed help. Adam darted down the path, and back to the cabin.

A stand of trees separated an overgrown field from a pond. Genesis sat at the control panel of her ship, **The Guardian.** She'd landed here after she'd watched lightning strike Dram's cruiser. His craft had burst into flames. She held her head in her hands and trembled.

"That was close. I could've been killed." The sight unnerved her. She forced herself out of her seat and switched off the controls. She had to find Dram and bring him back to headquarters, alive if possible.

She pulled the scanner from its holder. Her hands shook as she slipped the strap across her chest. Slow, deep breaths helped calm her.

This was the worst storm she had ever seen where bolts of electricity shot out of the sky. That rarely happened in the mountains on her planet, Atria. This field surrounded by woods reminded her of her home, a place she had not seen in ten *anos,* and she missed it.

She strapped a holster to her thigh and slipped the laser weapon inside. She knew what kind of animals lurked in the woods of Atria, but not here.

Beasts, larger and fiercer than those the men of her tribe hunted, showed in the database. The ancient ones had reported their findings after visiting this place thousands of *anos* ago.

She clipped Interplanetary Space Patrol issued hand restraints on the holster and opened The Guardian's hatch, stepping onto the ramp. A heavy rain fell. Thick *yetik* protected the scanner box from the elements, but not her. Within minutes, her *unicrin* was drenched.

Thank goodness her ship's earlier analysis of the atmosphere had showed the oxygen quality and content would sustain her, although the air held more contaminates than Atria's atmosphere. The difference was palpable.

She tapped the screen of the scanner's database and compared ancient reports with current information and displayed significant changes since the first visit. Blinking rain from her eyes, she aimed the scanner toward the crash site.

The heavier gravity slowed her movement, and the surrounding moisture smelled musty, reminding her of Persus.

She looked forward to the moment she would face Dram. He deserved to die for his crimes. But if he was killed in the accident, the location of her parents and the women of her village died with him. Under strict orders from the Interplanetary Space Patrol, she must bring Dram back alive to face his charges.

Failure of her mission meant the end of her tribe. Only men remained at White Mountain, unless they joined another tribe, or took mates from other villages to procreate. If Dram and his men hadn't captured the women and chil-dren while the men of her village had been hunting, she would be on Atria with her mate, raising a family of her own.

She touched the jeweled translator across her forehead and sighed. It was all she had left of her mother, Herda, besides her medallion. The heartbreaking memories brought a lump to her throat and her eyes watered. She should have run faster.

Herda had communicated with her telepathically until the distance between them had made it impossible.

She wiped the rain and sadness from her face, and rested her hand on the weapon. She wanted to kill Dram for what he had done.

Sharp-thorn vines grew throughout the woods with clusters of dark berries. Her hunger increased at the thought of eating the fruit. Her memory of the last real food she had eaten escaped her. The plants here seemed like those on Atria. She plucked one and inhaled the aroma. A purple stain formed on her fingers. She scanned the berry and read the results: 'Similar in structure to *nelu*, containing essential nutrients to sustain higher life forms.'

She popped several into her mouth. Mmmm. Not bad, and much sweeter than those from home.

Something crackled to her right, startling her. Her pulse quickened. The scanner indicated a large object running in her direction. Was it a beast or Dram?

Crouched behind a wide bush, her wet *unicrin* stuck to her skin, Genesis felt chilled as she peered above the foliage. A wooden dwelling stood in the distance to the left, beyond the pond. She let the scanner fall to her side. Grasping the weapon, she slowed her breathing as she eased the laser from the holster. Then she nudged the lever to stun with her forefinger. The rustling grew closer and her heart beat harder.

Adam ran through the woods. His pulse raced and his body filled with nervous energy. He had to get help. He could take the Jeep to the highway and make the call. Hopefully, the pilot was still alive.

Stories of aliens formed in his mind. He had read UFO sightings happened in fields in other states or along the coast of Florida, but not here in the Smokies. Knoxville had the closest military base.

Depictions in the newspapers had shown them resembling small, child-like creatures with large eyes. One story said they sucked the blood from cows in a field. UFOs fascinated him, but he'd never dreamed he would actually encounter one, let alone have it crash in his backyard.

The briars and vines scraped at his slicker and rubber boots, but tore through his jeans at the knees, causing sharp pain. He couldn't stop. Someone's life may depend on him.

Breathless, he considered calling the Sheriff's Department for help. But would they believe his story? Without them seeing the spaceship, he'd be put in a straitjacket. A report of a plane crash made more sense. Yeah, that's what he'd do. Then he'd call his boss, Jeremy. He could always count on Jeremy to come.

The sound of a branch breaking halted him in his tracks. His racing heart thudded twice before beating normally. He pulled the bow off his shoulder and fixed an arrow to the string. This was where he had seen the bear.

He glanced around and slowly stepped from the woods and onto the path by the pond. The rain had stopped now. The thick cloud cover obscured dawn's light. A heavy mist saturated the air, while fog rose over the water. In the soft mud, footprints, much smaller than his size eleven, headed toward his home. They came from the old cornfield he and his father had planted years ago. He had no neighbors, so no one else should be here. He turned toward the cabin. Maybe someone--

Another twig snapped behind him and he swung around, his bow fully drawn. He froze, aiming at the woman from his dream.

Did she come from the crash site? She didn't look like an alien, so who was she?

Her long, blue-black hair draped forward over one shoulder in a braid that came down to her waist. Her dark, tanned face stood out against the white jumpsuit she wore. White so bright it glowed. Her body gave the suit curves in all the right places, but her flawless skin accentuated furrowed brows and an expression that could kill.

On her forehead, a jeweled band made of a coppery-silver metal shimmered, and the jewels sparkled different colors. Straps across her shoulder attached to a box at her hip. She had a gun in one hand, pointed at his chest. His pulse quickened at the thought of being shot.

"Tannae se ut!" she shouted.

"What?" Adam cocked his head, his draw on the bow straining to release.

She tapped the band across her forehead with two fingers.

"Tannae se ut!" "Hold there, Dram!" she said.

Dram? "Hey, wait a minute," he lowered his bow slightly. "I'm Adam."

She shot a red beam of light from the weapon and hit the dead branch he stood on. The wood caught fire. He jumped and released his arrow between her feet.

"What the hell?" She meant to hurt him. Confusion and anxiety grabbed him as he nocked another arrow to the bowstring. She's got the wrong guy.

"Next one won't miss," she said, her eyebrows narrowed.

"Neither will I." His mouth went dry and he swallowed hard before responding again. "I'm not Dram. There's been an accident." He glanced in the direction of the crash. "I've got to get help."

"Drop the weapon," she ordered.

"Drop yours first!" With bears and aliens in the woods, he'd keep his bow and arrows.

She stepped closer and raised her pistol toward his face. He aimed his arrow for her heart, his own heart racing at the thought of killing someone. The branch she hit with the laser beam still burned and he didn't want the same thing happening to him.

"I said, drop the weapon." Her voice grew deeper and louder.

"Hell, no! Who are you and what are you doing on my property?" His anger gave rise to courage as he held his draw.

"So this is your base of operations?" She glanced around. "Who are you and why are you here?"

She lowered her weapon toward his chest and pulled the trigger.

He released his draw as a biting electrical shock flowed through him, paralyzing his extremities.

The woman dove away from the errant arrow as he fell

to his knees, then onto his face. "Ugh." He had heard about tasers but had never seen one. The cold, wet ground smelled moldy. He spat out dead, bitter leaves. She didn't appear to be a cop.

"Why...did you shoot me?" he moaned. He couldn't see her, but she tugged at his arms. He managed to turn his face a little.

"Are you there?" he called out. What's she doing?

"Get up," she ordered.

"Yeah, that's easy for you to say. How about giving me the taser and I'll use it on you." His arms and legs refused to obey him.

She pulled at his waist, drawing him back, as his face dragged across the wet, rocky ground. A tingling sensation began at his deltoids and moved down. She squeezed his shoulders, pulling him back, until all his weight rested on his knees. She kicked his boots.

"Get up!"

He brought one leg forward and pushed himself up,

then the other leg. He wobbled on his feet. Her grip tightened on his arms. Queasiness hit him in the gut. Behind him, his hands still tingled. Helplessness didn't suit him.

"What did you do to me?" He tried moving his upper body, and found his wrists were bound. Panic seized him.

"Go!" She pushed him forward.

"I'm not going anywhere until I get answers." He turned to face her, anger welling up. No one ordered him around, least of all someone he didn't know.

"You get questions answered when we arrive at headquarters."

She pushed him again.

"Are you an undercover cop or something?" He stumbled forward. Maybe he'd take her down in a wrestling hold he'd learned back in high school. That is, if his limbs returned to normal.

His rope coil hung across her chest. On one shoulder, she had his bow and quiver of arrows. She carried the taser she'd used on him. He clenched his jaw.

She pushed him in the direction of the cornfield.

"Go!" She gave him another shove. The tingling in his legs and arms faded.

"Wait just a minute! I'm not leaving unless you tell me what's going on."

She grabbed his wrists from behind and yanked up sharply.

He doubled over in pain. "Ouch! Damn that hurts."

She stuck the cold metal of the gun against his forehead as he straightened. His breath caught in his throat as he stared at the weapon. His heart beat so loudly, he heard the pulsing in his ears.

"I would love to finish you off now, but the I.S.P. wants to speak to you personally."

I.S.P.? He swallowed hard, his throat and mouth parched from the effort. He'd never heard of that agency. He took his gaze off the barrel momentarily and glanced into her dark, brown eyes framed in long lashes. Her brows furrowed in anger and her lips frowned.

"Look, I don't know what you're talking about, Scout's honor but I need to get help. There's been an accident and we're wasting time." He turned away, but she caught his restraints, twisted his wrists and immobilized him.

"Ouch. This has gone on long enough. Show me your I.D."

"What are you talking about? Go!" She waved her weapon at him.

He refused to move.

"Not until you tell me what's going on. And who are you, anyway?"

"You *will* go." She shoved him so hard he lost his balance, stumbling backward. He tripped over a dead tree in the path, falling on his backside.

"Oooof!" He glared up at her. He turned on his side to get up then froze when he saw it. Another space ship, only this one was whole. He recalled what he had seen earlier. There were two lights in the sky. Two space ships!

Genesis watched as Dram tried to get up from the wet ground. Her patience with him had ended. Now what? He stared at something through the underbrush. Exasperated, she bent down to locate the object of his attention. The Guardian? Before she could straighten, he wrapped his legs around her ankles and yanked her to the ground. She hit the dirt hard and the laser flew from her hand.

"Ugh!" She groped for the weapon. He threw himself on top of her, his body pressed against her breasts. She should kill him for his transgression.

"Look! There's the other spaceship. They're probably searching for the one that crashed. We've got to get help before the aliens show up. So quit this game you're playing and untie me."

Confusion engulfed her. He talked nonsense. His face, close to hers, breathed warmth against her cool skin. Blue eyes, wide with fear, captivated her and the heat from his body warmed her. Her pulse quickened, as a tingling rippled through her at light speed when their gazes met. They were motionless for an instant. His lips, inches from hers.

Her fingers found the laser. Good! She pulled it up to the side of his face. Anger infused her as she itched to fire the weapon. "Get off me now, or you will die right here." She tensed her jaw. Her carelessness had almost cost her. This man who had abducted both her parents and all the women from her village had abducted others as well. He deserved to die.

His legs straddled her as he used strong back muscles to pull himself up. He rolled off her and to the side where he rocked forward onto his hands, jamming his heels into the ground. He jumped to his feet in one motion. His gaze fixed on her as she scrambled to stand. She kept the weapon pointed at his head while he tensed his jaw.

How did he do that? "No more tricks!" She shouted as she waved the laser at him. Cautiously, she kept watch on him and gathered his things then pressed the hatch release button on the scanner.

Dram's gaze darted toward The Guardian and back to her. His eyes widened.

"Oh, my God, *you're* the...alien?" He stumbled backward.

She grabbed his shoulder to keep him upright. She couldn't let him escape now.

"Go." She turned him around to face The Guardian then 13

pushed him forward. He acted strange. Maybe he'd suffered brain damage after the crash.

She shoved the laser in his back as he moved toward the ship. He walked differently now and seemed dazed going up the ramp. She held his arm, guiding him inside.

The I.S.P. reported him as cocky and arrogant with no regard for authority. His injury must have changed his behavior. Ten long anos of searching for him was finally over.

She studied his yellow tunic, made of strange material she had never seen. It repelled water. She glanced at her own unicrin, the wet fabric stuck to her skin. Her body was chilled from the rain seeping through to her extremities.

Dram stopped when he reached the cage.

She pulled the *yav* from her scanner, zapping the lock mechanism and slid the heavy malloid door sideways. She shoved Dram inside.

Suddenly, a biting sting paralyzed her. Dizziness overtook her and she fell.

Numb with fear, Adam heard a body hit the floor. He swung around to find the woman at his feet. A man, wearing a light blue suit, like the woman's, hovered over her, taking the black box off her shoulder. He had her weapon in one hand, and another one in a thigh holster as he straightened and turned to face him.

His mouth dropped open in shock and his pulse quickened as the man facing him appeared a mirror image. From the white-blond hair, pale blue eyes and medium tan, to the same build and six-foot frame. The stranger stared back as he squinted to examine his face more closely. The older man had the beginnings of crows' feet where he did not. Did he smile or was that a smirk?

"You must be Dram."

"How did you know?"

"She mistook me for you." He glanced down at her still body. Did he hurt her? "Is she dead?" The thought bothered him more than he expected.

"No, but she will be when I get through with her."

Dram grabbed her arm and dragged her into the cell then turned to leave. He stepped over her, following Dram out, but Dram shoved him back.

"Sorry, boy." He slammed the door shut.

"Hey, wait! I don't belong here. The whole thing is a big mistake."

"Actually, everything is working out perfectly." Dram raised one blond eyebrow and smirked again. He hesitated before picking up his possessions then stowed them in some kind of compartment.

He watched as anger boiled inside. "Be careful with my stuff." His father had taught him how to hunt and his bow and arrows were all he had left of his dad.

Dram ignored him and headed toward a door. He turned back and pressed a button on the black box. "You won't need those anymore." The ramp to the ship closed as Dram entered the other room. Dazed, he watched as the opening hissed shut behind Dram.

He glanced around the interior of the vessel as his gut tightened in fear. "God, help me."

Shiny metal, like new stainless steel, covered everything including the floor, the ceiling, and the walls. Inside, the place seemed round. Outside, it had appeared football shaped. Three doors, evenly spaced apart, stood across from the main entrance. The one Dram walked through was on the far right of the cell. On the far left was a pedestal table, encircled by two benches. Compartments of various sizes lined the walls on either side of his prison.

Between the left lockers and his cage was a large circle flush with the floor. It took up space with a man-hole cover of sorts. No hinges or handle adorned it. Above that spot, in the ceiling, another similar shape existed.

He leaned against the bars and closed his eyes. He should have stayed in bed this morning. Two of his visions had come true. The first time he'd had premonitions, his life had changed drastically, making him an orphan. And now this had happened.

He shook his head. Loneliness he could deal with. Only God knew what would happen now. He felt nauseous and wanted to puke.

Lord, don't let me end up a science experiment for aliens.

His twenty-six-year life flashed before his eyes. Memories of his family, days at the orphanage, right up to his current construction job, working for his friend, Jeremy. He liked his job, too.

Suddenly, a quiet hum started, causing a light vibration under his feet. *We're moving.* His life had just changed. He lowered his head.

He noticed the young woman sprawled out across the metal floor. He let his tired, hungry body slide slowly to the ground. He understood how she had mistaken him for Dram. To share the face of a total stranger seemed uncanny, especially an alien. How ironic, though, that the man she thought she'd captured had turned around and abducted her. Now they both suffered the same fate.

Her dirty, drenched white suit clung to her unconscious body, showing off luscious curves and bare skin underneath.

"Hmmm." *How interesting.* He leaned closer to get a better view. *Why hadn't he noticed before?*

His flesh was chilled because he wore jeans soaked at the knees and a sweatshirt wet around the neck. He turned sideways, pried off his muddy boots, and wriggled his toes. Then, sitting cross-legged, he leaned against the bars and realized he had no other shoes when the air cooled his feet.

Thoughts of things he'd left behind on Earth like his fishing poles, cabin, and Jeep, crossed his mind. He banged his head against the bars. Would he ever return home again? He thought he had problems with a clingy girlfriend and a stray cat. When Jeremy comes over later this morning to go fishing, he won't be there. Would Jeremy search for him?

In the Navigation room, Dram straightened in his chair. Thank goodness the storm had dissipated. Flying in bad weather had been difficult. He lifted a lever then tapped 'location' on the keypad of the Nav-U-Com.

The monitor flashed astronomical charts across the screen until stopping on one with ten planets. He punched in 'system?' The display showed: 'SSO, or star system one. Two questionable, might be moons.'

"Great," he mumbled, as he typed in 'location within system?' Twenty-seven *anos* had passed since his last visit. He smiled and his heart lightened at the memories while the monitor displayed: 'third planet from unnamed star.'

"Now you're talking," he said. He identified 'Earth' for the database. His fingers flew across the keys, spelling 'escape trajectory?' The display showed Earth and changing graphics of a window outside the planet. It aimed at the star with coordinates listed above the drawings.

He typed 'enhancement' to get a closer view.

Hmmm, what had Emma called it? He entered 'sun' for the

database then hit the keys and spelled 'Plexus?' His mind briefly reflected on the only woman he had ever loved.

The coordinates appeared along with the wormholes and trajectory through hyperspace from the sun.

He punched in 'window' and the graphics displayed once more, aiming at the sun. He set the destination for its gravity well, entering the parameters, and then pulled back on the controls. The ship lifted off the ground 300 *centikiks*. He pointed the ovoidal shape toward the giant star.

Relieved, he settled in his seat, his clothes sodden from his recent ordeal. He would have to find something to change into once he left the Earth's gravity. He glanced around the Nav-room. State of the art technology, compliments of the Interplanetary Space Patrol. *How nice.* Their seal was stamped on the center of the console. No doubts as to owner- ship. *How did the woman get a ship like this?* Unless she worked for them. She seemed a little young to recruit into service.

He clasped his hands behind his head and remembered sadly the times he and his partner, Timna, had close calls with the I.S.P. But Timna no longer had to worry about them. One minute he'd controlled the ship, the next, Timna was dead. Luckily, he'd survived.

He gazed out the view port at the sun. Until he got within this system, he hadn't realized someone pursued him. Emma called this the solar system.

He and Timna had tried to shake off their pursuer, but nothing had worked. *Why would a lone, young woman chase them, anyway?*

How ironic that she'd found the very person he had come to find, thinking the man from Earth was him. *Perfect.* She seemed convinced of the boy's identity. Perhaps others could be, too. The boy resembled him more than he had anticipated. Now hopeful, he had to create a flawless plan.

Already behind schedule, he had to return to his base on Meta to get the last shipment out to Z. If Z didn't approve the merchandise, his business was *kunnarled.* Hmmm. An idea formed in his brain. He just might succeed with the boy's help.

Back in the cell, Adam yanked and wriggled his wrists in frustration. Whatever the woman had used to bind them, held fast. He couldn't reach his Swiss Army knife in his jeans pocket. If she woke, maybe she'd help him.

He thought of Dram again and how disturbing it was to share features with a man not related. He was an only child, something he and his parents had in common. No chance Dram could be related. He shook his head. He had to get those thoughts out of his mind. Both of them were aliens, yet they appeared human. When he was on top of her, though, she'd had all the right equipment.

Did they have red blood? Maybe a star out there had a twin to everyone on Earth? *Was it possible two planets shared the same history or God?*

He was taught that God had created the universe and everything in it. Perhaps God didn't stop with Earth. What if He made men on other planets as well? It would be a waste to set people in just one place when He initially had so many stars and galaxies.

God meant for him to meet this woman. Otherwise, why have that premonition?

Stories of aliens looking less than human must be true, too. Somebody had witnessed them, hadn't they?

Confused, he leaned his head against the bars of the cell. He had too much to think about now.

He heard the woman stir. Her lids fluttered open, and her lips moved.

"Malek?" Her eyes widened at the sight of him.

"What?" He leaned closer to hear her.

She lunged for his throat.

"Whoa!" He fell back as her hands squeezed tight around his neck, his airway closing off. He twisted and turned, trying to shake her loose, but she held firm. Her weight, pressing against him, knocked him off balance and he rolled to his side. He flipped to his back. He didn't want to die. Not now. Not this way. He had to survive.

Something struck him in the face while she pressed harder on his throat. A couple of medallions dangled in front of him. Both identical and shaped like trees encircled in metal. They hung around her neck with long leather straps.

He remembered a wrestling maneuver and drew his knees tight to his chest. He wedged his feet between him and her soft body, beneath her breasts. Then he forced his legs out straight, shooting her across the small cell. She slammed into the bars opposite him.

She sat there, dazed. Her eyes were wide in surprise. Two large footprints were imprinted on her outfit, just under each breast.

He rolled onto his side, coughing and gagging. He coughed so hard, he heaved, almost puking. He managed to roll into a kneeling position, his head against the floor.

"I am not Dram!" His voice was hoarse.

He pulled himself up and sat back on his heels, wiping his mouth on the shoulder of his rain slicker.

"Dram is flying this space ship." The awful taste would not go away. "Dram..." He coughed again, anger infused him. "Dram put you in here!"

"You tricked me," she said, glaring at him.

"Yeah, well if I was Dram, how did I knock you out? My hands are tied behind my back." He twisted his body around to show her his bound wrists, aching from the restraints.

"And," he continued. "I certainly wouldn't be in this cage with you!" he snapped. "I had a life on Earth before you came along. You've changed everything!"

Her eyes narrowed as she glared at him. She pulled her knees up to her chest and lowered her head.

"Your fate could be worse, Earth man," she replied, tensing her jaw. Her brows deeply furrowed.

"Oh, yeah? What could be worse than being abducted from my home?" He tightened his fists, irritating the raw areas under the restraints.

"I could have *killed* you," she whispered harshly.

A scene from the moon, Ti, which takes place in The Abduction

View of Meta from Dram's base on Meta

3

DELETED SCENE FROM REVENGE

Tarsius

She had been sick since Mariposa was born and without a healer in our village, it didn't look good. I helped her take care of the baby as much as I could for a boy of seven. Mama had powers but they weren't the kind of powers that could heal. She was respected in our village, so a couple went to seek a healer when she first became ill. That was many moon cycles ago.

Papa went to work in the shipyard as usual that morning. Later that afternoon, I prepared a soup for dinner.

While Mariposa played on the floor, I practiced my skills of moving objects with my mind. Suddenly, there was a commotion outside with women screaming. I ran to see what happened.

"Stay inside, Berto! Something bad is happening, I can feel it," Mama said.

Papa didn't come home that night and Mama wouldn't eat.

"Take care of Mariposa, Berto. Don't let anything happen to her." Mama closed her eyes.

"Mama, eat something," I pleaded. She didn't answer me, so I shook her to wake her up. But Mama didn't wake up.

The next morning, I packed a few things in a bag, put Mariposa in her backpack, and we left the only home we ever knew.

Denoy, Tarsius, Berto's home planet (Deposit Photos)

Excerpt from Revenge

Denoy, Planet Tarsius

Mariposa frowned at Berto. "Did you get in trouble today at the Academy?"

Berto sat by the fire pit, cooking a wild taffit bird on a makeshift spit. He tore off a leg and handed it to his sister. "Don't eat the bones, Mariposa, and no, I didn't get in trouble." He took a bite of taffit. The juices from the succulent bird dripped down his chin. He wiped it off with the back of his hand. He was hungrier than he thought. The sweet aroma of the roasting bird had his stomach growling but the luscious taste made him forget how he had to live.

"I saw you talking to Headmaster Torres." She took a bite of the leg, glancing up at him.

"Headmaster Torres found a job for me. I start tomorrow after classes. I'll learn how to fix wing ships, then maybe cargo ships."

"What about me? Who is going to watch me while you're gone?"

He bowed his head. Seven anos was too young to leave alone, but he had been orphaned at that age with an infant sister to take care of.

"Promise me you'll stay here in the cave when you get finished with classes."

"Aren't you going to walk me home?" She bit her lower lip and raised her brows.

"Mari, I would, but the job is on the other side of Denoy. I would be late getting to work."

Mari pouted, on the verge of tears.

"Look, Mari, it's only for one day. I'll ask my new boss if you can come with me. You can study while I work."

"Can't I go with you tomorrow?"

"No, Mari. I have to speak to the boss first to make sure it's okay. Now, eat your taffit."

Later, he tucked her into the makeshift bed of reeds and palms with a blanket he had stolen years before. He looked forward to the day he could pay for his food. When he couldn't catch anything to eat, he'd stolen it.

He washed up by the small waterfall that trickled into a shallow pool. The coolness of the cave and the smell of wet rock was constant and kept out the heat of the day. The cave had been their home since he was seven. He curled up on the mat beside Mari's and went to sleep.

The next morning, he dressed in the only clothes he owned —ragged pants and a stained shirt along with his worn-out sandals. Mari's dress was short and tattered and her sandals no longer fit. Soon he would be able to buy her some clothes.

After gathering wood for the fire pit, he showed her how to use her energy to make a spark. Several tries later, Mari succeeded.

"Can I make the fire when I get home?" she asked excitedly.

"I'll help you gather more wood so you'll have enough."

Their home was at the base of Dos Santos Mountains, hidden in the forest where there were plenty of dead branches to gather. The main trail through Denoy led to the next village, but the trail to their cave was concealed by trees and thick underbrush. He placed the kindling they gathered against the far wall of the cave.

He walked with Mari to the Academy through the woods as usual. He heard the birds chirping and small animals scurrying under brush. Denoy was set in a clearing, surrounded by the forest on three sides and the mountains on the other. Vaedra, their sun, was bright and warm as always in a cloudless sky. The homes were all dome-shaped brownish-red dwellings clustered on either side of a dirt road in the center. The road led from the forest and ended at the shipyards near the Academy. One of those homes used to be theirs.

He had to beg the Headmaster to let him bring Mari to class with him when she was an infant. He explained to Torres their only aunt lived in Eloy, another village on

Tarsius. He hadn't seen her since before his mother died and didn't know how to contact her.

It took a while for Mari to adjust but the instructors had given him plenty of latitude when they learned his mother had died and his father disappeared on the same day. Eventually, the instructors got used to having Mari around.

The day dragged on. His studies held no interest for him. All he thought about was the chance for a better life and learning some new skills. Finally, the alarm sounded and the classes dispersed. He spotted Mari, heading down the steps of the brownish-red colored building. He hurried to her.

"Mari!"

She turned at the sound of her name.

"Go straight home and stay in the back of the cave, Mari."

"I will. When will you come home?"

"I'll be there before dark. You can start the fire just before then." Their lives would be different after today. Maybe soon they would have a dwelling to call home, instead of a cave.

He squatted down and hugged her. "I'll be home as soon as I can. I love you, Mari."

"I love you, too, Berto."

He raced to the area that once housed a thriving ship building business. Some time ago, something happened that caused them to stop production. Ignacio's Repair Shop was just before the gated entrance to the Denoy Ship Yards.

"You must be Berto," a short, round man said. Ignacio's tan was darker than his own.

"Yes, sir. Headmaster Torres sent me."

"Come, let me show you my shop." Ignacio pointed out the sections of the shop where certain work was performed.

There were women and boys, slightly older than himself, working in all the areas. The first was the navigation section, then a thruster section. Another section was devoted to cooling and heating, another for life support systems, and the main section was for engine systems.

"Since production was halted at the shipyards, I've been busy repairing all the old ships. I'll start you off with the thruster section. I expect you to be here every day until dark. You get paid once a week. Do you have a place to stay?"

"For tonight, sir."

"There's Community housing over there." He pointed to a tall, dome-shaped light brown building across the way. "They serve two meals a day. Do you have any questions?"

"Uh, yes sir. I have a younger sister that I'm responsible for. I was wondering if I could...well...bring her to work with me? I promise she won't be any trouble. She's quiet and she'll study while I work."

Ignacio studied him. "What about your parents?"

"It's just me and Mari."

"How have you survived?"

"I'd rather not say, sir, but we've managed. I really need this job."

"You hiding something, boy. Doing anything...illegal?"

"No sir. It's just...I don't want to leave Mari alone. She's too young."

"Torres said you were a hard worker. I'm willing to give you a chance. All right, be here after classes tomorrow— both of you. Maybe I can find something for her to do as well."

"Yes, sir! You won't regret this. Thank you, sir." He shook hands with Ignacio and hurried out the door.

Berto ran as fast as he could through the village to the

path in the woods that led to the cave they called home. As he approached the rocky cliffs, he thought he heard muffled sounds. When he got to the mouth of the cave, darkness had settled over the forest.

A piercing scream cut through his heart. Mari!

The dim glow from the fire showed three shadowy figures about his size, leaning over something...Mari!

Oh God! One held her arms down, another held her legs. A third person was on top of her, trying to rape her. The boy's white-blond hair and blue eyes marked him as Chromian.

"No!" Berto's shout echoed throughout the cave as his anger and adrenalin surged through his body, his gut tightening. He lunged for the boy on top, but the energy built up inside him shot out through his hands before he reached him, throwing the boy across the cave, slamming his head against the wall.

As his rage built, his adrenalin pumped faster throughout his body. He reached for the boy holding down Mari's arms, the energy surged again, throwing the boy against another wall. The boy hit the rock hard then slumped over.

He glared at the last boy, who held Mari's legs, moving toward him. He fisted his hands at his sides to keep from doing more harm, but the boy ran out of the cave. The last boy and the second one, with their brown skin and eyes, were Tarsian, like himself and Mari, but he didn't recognize either of them.

He scooped up Mari and hugged her tight. She clung to him, weeping. His heart pounded from the ordeal. His mind was dizzy with comprehension of his newly discovered skill. He had only pulled things toward himself or started fires with his power but this was new. He could feel Mari's body trembling...or was that him?

"Mari, I promise, I will never leave you alone again."

They were no longer safe here. He helped her dress, gathered the few belongings they had, and left the cave, carrying her in his arms.

Shipyards outside Denoy, Tarsius, where Berto worked (Deposit Photos)

View of Meta from other side of the mountains (Deposit Photos)

4

———

INTERVIEWS

Adam Davis Interview

"So tell me, Adam, how did you meet Genesis?"

"It was an accident. No, I take that back. It was fate."

"How do you mean?"

"Well, it was storming and storms make me uncomfortable."

"Why is that?"

"My parents were killed in a car accident during a thunder storm. Anyway, I was tossing and turning, trying to sleep, when I had a premonition."

"What kind of premonition?"

"Well, first there was the space ship which I thought was a plane. The second was a vision of a beautiful woman dressed in white, which was Genesis. The third was the struggle I would face between me and Dram."

"Did you understand all this at the time?"

"No. I figured it out as I went. I never dreamed I would be abducted by aliens. I mean, who would, right?"

"Right."

"I didn't even get it until I was forced onto the spaceship. She looked like any woman you would meet on Earth. I was thinking little gray guys with big eyes, you know? Not some gorgeous Native American woman."

"So what did you do when you figured it out?"

"There was nothing I **could** do. I freaked out at first, thinking I would be experimented on, but I was tied up with some type of plastic. I couldn't break free."

"Didn't you try to run?"

"What? And get fried by her laser gun? She had good aim, let me tell you."

"What happened after she got you on the ship?"

"That's when I met Dram. He shot her with the stun gun and knocked her out. When I turned around, she was on the ground."

"What was it like, meeting Dram?"

"It was freaky seeing my face on somebody I didn't know. Especially an alien! It was like looking in the mirror except the mirror was doing something different than I was."

"I bet that was weird. So what happened?"

"Well, he dragged Genesis into the cage and I followed him out but he shoved me back in and slammed the cage door."

"That doesn't sound good."

"No, it wasn't. He turned and left me there. I think my life passed before my eyes. I got this sick in the gut feeling. I felt...helpless. A feeling I never want to feel again."

"So what did you do?"

"I was a prisoner in a cage. There wasn't anything I could do. Then Genesis woke up."

"So she was now a prisoner as well?"

"Yes, only she didn't realize it at first. She tried to kill me with her bare hands. She almost succeeded until I remembered a wrestling hold I used in high school."

"Did that save you?"

"Yes and it got her off me real quick."

Genesis Interview

"So, Genesis, how did you meet Adam Davis?"

"I had been searching for Dram for ten anos. I thought I had finally captured him but it turned out...I had the wrong man."

"That must have been very disappointing for you."

"Yes, it was. I thought I would finally see my village of women, my mother, and my father's mother."

"So, what did you do when you discovered the error?"

"I apologized...eventually. Then he did something strange."

"What was that?"

"He forgave me."

"That was a nice gesture."

"Yes, but it stunned me. He even offered to help me find my father. What do you say to someone like that? I mean, I almost killed him."

"But you didn't."

"Almost. I wanted to kill him for what he did to my village and then I remembered my error. I could have killed an innocent man!"

"Did he help you?"

"Yes, he did."

Berto Interview

"Hello, Berto! Can you tell me how you met Adam Davis?"

"I met him on Dram's base on Meta."

"Did he say much to you while you were both there?"

"Not at first. It was strange to see a younger version of Dram on base. You had to get close to see that is was Adam and not Dram."

"How could you tell the difference?"

"Around the eyes, Adam looked younger. Then later I discovered he grew hair on his face."

"And you don't?"

"No. No one in the Vaedra System does either. We grow hair on our heads and our eyebrows, that's it."

"That's interesting. How did you come to know Dram?"

"Four anos ago, I partnered with Bordon to steal a cargo transport."

"Why?"

"I needed the kashis and he knew where to find a ship. We had boarded the transporter with no problem. When we got everything ready for take-off, I went into the Nav Room and Dram was there, holding a laser pistol. He ordered me to sit and navigate to where he directed me."

"Was that the first time you met him?"

"Yes. He gave me an option, though."

"And what was that?"

"I could work for him or he would kill me."

Cargo Transport (Deposit Photos) Berto helped to steal

5

——————

DELETED SCENE FROM BETRAYED

Admiral Esrith sat in his command chair looking out the forward viewport of the Concordance as the ship came out of hyper-speed. In front of him to his left was the Navigator's station and to his right, the Captain's station. Behind him to his right was Communications and to his left, an observation post, where Adam Davis, Genesis, and Tremol stood, looking out the massive viewport.

"Captain Melbus, what is our position?"

The Captain examined his charts and glanced up at the viewport. "I believe we are approaching the planet Mars, sir, according to the Earth man."

"Set our heading toward Earth, Captain Melbus," the Admiral responded.

Suddenly, a beam of light flashed from one of the moons toward the ship.

"Shields up, Captain Melbus!"

"Aye sir!"

Another beam of light hit the right side of the ship, followed by several more shots.

"What's happening?" Adam asked, leaning toward the viewport.

"It looks like there's a small contingent of ships by that second moon," Captain Melbus answered him.

"Do we take evasive action, sir?" Captain Melbus looked to the Admiral.

"Get a lock on their position and fire back, Captain."

"Aye sir!"

"Locked on," first officer Akania responded.

"Fire!" Captain Melbus called out.

"I thought Mars was uninhabited," the Admiral stated.

"I thought so too, sir. I mean, the only thing I knew that was on Mars was the rover."

"What is a rover?" The Admiral asked.

The ship took a couple more hits from the moon and shook lightly.

"Fire again!" Melbus called out.

"The Mars Rover is a robotic vehicle searching Mars for life, collecting samples for scientists to study back on Earth. At least that's what the government has been telling us," Adam said.

"Fire again," Melbus called out. "It doesn't look like we're stopping them, sir."

"Are your people doing something on one of the moons?" the Admiral said.

"Not that I know of sir. We don't have the technology on Earth for space ships like those."

"How strong is your military space force?" The Admiral asked.

"I don't think we have one, sir."

"You don't have a military presence in space?"

"No sir, unless you count the astronauts."

"And what are those?"

"They're pilots of the rockets we've sent into space."

The Admiral stood. "Captain Melbus, take evasive action, keeping the shields up."

A few more blasts hit the shields, shaking the command center.

"Aye sir. Evasive action, now!" Captain Melbus called out.

"Evasive action," Lanka, the Navigator, announced.

"We don't want to start a war between your people and Mars if you can't defend yourselves."

"Yes, sir. I mean, no we don't."

"Who would be shooting at us, Adam?"

"That's a good question, sir."

"Set the course for Earth, Captain Melbus."

"Course is set, sir."

Main Deck of the Concordance (Deposit Photos)

Days Later

"We're coming into the moon's gravity field, sir," Captain Melbus reported.

Adam, Genesis and Tremol stood behind Melbus, gazing

out the viewport.

"I've never been this close to the moon before," Adam said. "This must be the dark side of the moon."

As they moved closer, he could see what looked like dwellings.

"What the..."

"Nice village," Captain Melbus responded. "Is that your moon base?"

"Uh, that's not ours, sir."

"What do you mean? Whose base is it?" Tremol asked.

"That's a good question. I know our astronauts landed on the moon years ago but never went back after a couple of landings. They just collected rock samples and came back."

"Maybe your Earth people are not ready for our technology," Admiral Esrith said.

"I'm beginning to wonder, sir. It seems we are so behind that if that village on the moon isn't ours or those ships on the moon of Mars, then there's no way we could defend ourselves against aliens from other planets."

"You were able to convince the Council of Nations on Vestra. I think you can do the same for your planet," Counselor Contor said.

"Thanks Counselor. I hope you're right."

Earth's Moon Base (Deposit Photos)

The Next Day

"Genesis, I want you to stay on the ship, just in case something happens to me," Adam said. He wrapped his arms around her. "And I told Tremol to watch over you."

"And what would happen to you?"

"Well, after being shot at from the moon of Mars, I'm thinking the government hasn't been up front with its people."

Genesis cocked her head.

"I don't trust the government, Gen."

"I see."

"You and Tremol will be my back up if something does happen."

"I don't understand," she said.

"I can communicate with you if I can't use the communicators that the officers wear." He reached for Genesis' comm-pad. "Here, I'll write down Jeremy's phone number," he said. He put in his boss' phone number and address and then added his own address before handing the comm-pad back to her.

"The Admiral is sending Counselors Contor, Thebes, me, and a pilot to talk to the scientists at NASA."

"When will you be leaving?" Genesis asked.

"In about an hour or so. I love you, Gen." He pulled her close and kissed her. She pulled him closer and returned the kiss. He didn't want to leave her alone on this large ship with mostly males aboard, but the thought of sharing all this technology is what brought him back to Earth in the first place.

"Do you have the communicator that Malik made for you?" she asked.

He pulled it out from his shirt. "Yes. Are you wearing yours?"

She nodded.

"If it turns out that NASA is not where we need to go, we'll head to the White House and try to speak to the President."

Genesis cocked her head again.

"He's the leader of our country."

She nodded before pulling him into another hug.

"Ready to go?" the pilot asked, approaching them.

Adam turned to see Counselors Contor and Thebes behind the pilot.

"Sure."

The three of them boarded the dome-shaped ship, similar to the one Genesis flew when she abducted him months ago.

It took him that long to convince the Council of Nations to share their technology with Earth. It certainly couldn't hurt to have alliances with the people in the Vaedra System. After all, they were willing to sell Earth some space ships and exchange scientists and medical people to teach and learn from each other.

"Everyone strap in," the pilot ordered. "I'm Eno, by the way."

He sat beside Eno in the co-pilot seat. "Need help in pre-flight?" he asked.

"Sure."

The two of them checked the systems and when completed, Eno got clearance for takeoff out of hangar bay four.

"Earth Mission One, clear to go."

Ship heading to Earth from the Concordance (Deposit Photos)

Excerpt from Betrayed

PLANET EARTH

WASHINGTON, D.C.

Was it wrong to pray that nothing happened every day? Keely McGuire sat in the back of the briefing room

while Gowan went over assignment changes. She prayed her assignment stayed the same. She had been at the White House a year now and still felt like a rookie. Gowan had finished talking and hadn't called her name. While other agents got up to leave, she headed to the front of the room to check her assignment. Gowan spoke to another agent away from the desk. She ran her finger down the page. Good. She was assigned to the Oval Office again today.

A heavy hand rested on her shoulder. She straightened and turned. Gowan.

"Yes, you still have Oval Office duty." "Thank you, sir," she managed to say. "I'm surprised, McGuire."

"Oh?"

"Most agents look forward to a change in duty at least

every now and then. Sometimes they even ask for a change, but not you. Why is that?"

"I like where I'm at, sir."

"Do you, McGuire?"

She swallowed hard and nodded. She couldn't get away fast enough. When she got to the Oval Office, she straightened her bulletproof vest and checked her holster to make sure her Sig was in place. She didn't care that other agents got promotions or moved on to other assignments. She liked where she was. It was safe.

When her shift ended, she offered another prayer of thanks for an uneventful day. She checked her watch. Her parents had invited her over for the weekend. She hadn't seen them in a month and looked forward to the visit.

Her cell phone rang as she got into her car.

"Hello, David, how was your day?" she asked.

"I got a new lead on a story I've been working on. How about you? Did you wear that new ring I bought you?"

"My day was quiet as usual. I'm sorry, but I forgot to wear the ring. I promise I'll wear it next week."

"Good. Be sure that you do. I just can't believe you work at the White House and nothing ever happens around there."

"I'm sure things happen there, I'm just not at the scene where it does."

"Is this the weekend you're heading into Virginia to see your parents?"

"Yes. Would you like to join me? I'm sure they'd love to meet you."

"Maybe some other time. I'll be hanging out with the boys this weekend. You have fun. I'll see you when you get back."

Keely set her phone in the seat next to her then pulled

off her vest. Although she had been seeing David for nearly a month, she didn't feel comfortable sharing what her career entailed. After all, he worked for a local newspaper, writing about life in Washington, DC. She was a Secret Service agent and secrets were part of her life. Their motto was "Worthy of Trust and Confidence." She wasn't sure how much she could trust David yet. As far as David knew, she was an intern in the Office of Public Liaison through the White House internship program. She actually had worked there briefly while waiting to be accepted by the Secret Service.

It was probably good that he decided not to take her up on her offer. Her mother didn't like him, and she hadn't even met him.

She put the top down on her convertible and pulled her hair loose from the tight bun she wore while she worked. Since she had packed her bags earlier this morning, she headed south to Virginia. This weekend she had to tell them she was having second thoughts on her career choice.

6

───────

INTERVIEW WITH CAPTAIN TREMOL

Today I'm speaking with Captain Tremol of the newly formed Earthen Delegation to the Vaedra System. Hello Captain Tremol. Can you tell us a little about what your job entails?

Of course. I'm one of the new liaisons, leading a group of dignitaries from your Earth to Vaedra's planet, Vestra Major, which is our home planet in the system. I'm from Vestra Major as well. I will set up accommodations for these people and line up introductions to their counter parts in our system so they can learn from each other.

That sounds like a good idea. How did that position come about?

Well, after Keely helped me find my missing landing party on Earth, her president came aboard our ship for a visit. He like the idea of sharing technology and assigned Keely for the Vaedran Delegation and me for the Earthen part. Since Keely knows the Earth and I'm from the Vaedra System, we were perfect choices.

Tell me Captain, do you celebrate any holidays in the Vaedra System?

We have our Independence Day on all the planets. That's

when all the various cultures got their own planets in which to live. We also celebrate the New Ano and all the solstices. Of course, each planet has their ano ending at different times and their solstices are also at different times depending on where Vaedra is in relation to their seasons. Lastly, we celebrate the birth of our Lord. On Vestra Major, that was just after our winter solstice. I believe each planet holds its celebration in their winter solstice as well, but some planets have 14 moon cycles and others may have twelve or less, so the date changes for each planet.

That's interesting. Do you have special activities that you do on these holidays?

On the Independence Day, all cultures celebrate with feasting and dancing with great fireworks at night. With the solstices, mostly it depends on the culture. On Vestra Major, where I'm from, the family gathers for an evening meal and tells stories of antics from past solstices. If the families are far apart, then this is a time for visiting and merriment. But on the Lord's Day, we go to our churches and celebrate his birth with friends and family, giving gifts of food or clothing to those less fortunate than ourselves.

That sounds interesting as well. We have some similarities in our celebrations. Thank you Captain, for taking time with me today.

7

———

EXCERPT FROM AFTERMATH

Atlantic Ocean, Off the Coast of Florida

"I got a big one, Dad!"

"Fight it, Jimmy. Don't lose it. Eddie, get the gaff hook."

Eddie moved behind his brother to grab the gaff. A strange light, moving rapidly underwater toward their boat, caught his attention. What would be out here late at night? Eddie pulled out his phone and started filming it.

Dave moved behind Jimmy to help him hold onto the pole. "Eddie! Where's that gaff hook?"

"Dad! Look at this!" Eddie shouted.

Dave glanced toward Eddie. The ocean lit up around the boat. Dave was thrown off balance as Jimmy fell into his arms. One hand was around his son, the other held the pole. Dave swung his attention to the bow of the boat as it lifted out of the water. He and Jimmy fell back against the cabin. The giant grouper fell on top of Jimmy, thrashing and kicking. Before them, a space ship wider than six cabin cruisers lifted out of the water with two more ships on each side of it.

Their boat slammed back into the water.

"Eddie? Are you all right?"

"I got it, Dad! I got it on my phone."

Before he could show his dad the film, more lights came toward them from under the ocean.

Eddie turned around and filmed it. This time, the space ships did not lift the boat, but came out farther ahead of them in the water. These five ships were about the same size as the first five.

"Call the Coast Guard, Dad," Jimmy said.

"Who is going to believe it, son?"

Eddie took a picture of Jimmy with his fish. "I sent it to the local news. They'll believe the film footage, Dad. This is news!"

Altay Mountains, Russia

A group of hikers on an outing looked up at the mountains and saw six UFOs fly out from the mountain range and head up into space. One of the hikers pulled out his camera and took pictures of the ships before they disappeared.

Virginia Countryside

Mr. and Mrs. McGuire sat in their living room and watched the news reports about the alien exodus.

"I think we should go and stay at Keely's apartment in D.C.," Mrs. McGuire said.

"Why? We've had the implants taken out."

"Yes, but they may still find us. They know where we live."

Mr. McGuire stood up. "You're right, honey. We better start packing."

Situation Room, White House, Washington, DC

"The latest reports from around the world shows a mass exodus of space ships heading into space. Here are some images from Russia. Then we have some from the Pacific

Ocean and the Mediterranean Sea. The last is a video from the coast of Florida."

The President and his key officials watched the screen as a newscaster reported. The president sat forward in his seat. "Has General Yermolay decided to talk?"

"He's talking to his lawyer, sir," his aide replied.

"This secret government stops now. This thing Truman started has snowballed into a giant mess. Now we have these aliens, living on our planet, secretly working with a select few for the benefit of that select few. I want answers and I want them now. If we have to arrest everyone involved to get answers, then so be it. The future of this planet is at stake and it all falls back on this secret government."

"I believe the DOJ have arrested about forty people so far, sir."

"Someone needs to start talking. The aliens are planning something and it doesn't look good."

Space, The Concordance

Captain Gadara ni Hovsep sat at her Nav-U-Comm, watching the six pilots take turns landing their class A wing ships, otherwise known as military escorts, into the Concordance's landing bays.

"Easy and steady. There you go. Good job! Next!"

She could see the four remaining pilots holding behind the Concordance, waiting their turns.

She had already taught them how to fly the wedges and these military escort ships. All that was left were the transporters. When this group finished their tour with the Concordance, she would finally get her promotion to Mission Specialist and be in the next Exploration Group, leaving the Vaedra System. She had done everything she set out to do with the military. Anything higher than Captain in the military meant more paperwork and she refused to do any more of that. Now, she wanted more action.

She wanted to see what else was out there. The Earth system seemed interesting enough, but that planet was well populated. Did they even explore their own system? Were there people on the other planets rotating around their sun?

She didn't get her questions answered because she had been training these six new pilots for the Vaedran Military. While Admiral Esrith had the Concordance hovering over Earth, waiting for his mission to end, she had her own mission.

These pilots seemed ready. They took all the sim training and manual training she gave them. This last part was actual flight training maneuvers, most of it spent flying around Earth and its moon. Every scenario she could think of, she threw at them, and they handled it well. They tried landings on Earth's oceans and on the moon's surface. It was tense for a while when they lost communications on the moon. And being fired at by those lunar people gave her pilots some live escape practice. Were those lunar people the same people who lived on Earth? Why did they shoot at them? They were just practicing landings on rough surfaces. If their communications hadn't been jammed, the lunar people would have known that.

She was anxious to talk to Eno and find out how the Earth pilots did with their brief training. Were they difficult to work with? Were they fast learners? After his rescue, he took some of the best Vaedran pilots to Earth to train their best pilots.

There was one more flight scheduled for her trainees, but that would be after they made the jump. It would be landing at the Timucan Space Station between Vestra Major and Persus. They had already practiced space jumps, so she was looking forward to the landing. Space station landings could be tricky. Once they passed this test, the rest was all about flight time. If they wanted promotions, they needed to fly more.

Now, she looked forward to some time off. And a tall drink. It was her turn to land. She pulled into the hanger as the Concordance closed up the landing ramp. She waited for pressurization before opening her door.

The rest of her crew gathered around her ship, waiting for orders.

"Okay guys, you're off the next two days. Report to our Sim Room at 0900 hours on Monday."

"Yes!" A couple shouted from the group.

"And don't be late!" She couldn't get out of there fast enough. She still had to write up the reports on each man and how they performed for this part of their training. But that could wait. Drink first, paperwork later.

Gadara headed to the Officers Lounge on deck 1. She checked her chrono. It was early. She wouldn't have to put up with anyone at this hour. Most officers showed up after the evening meal.

She took the stairs. The people movers were too slow for her. She had energy to burn and this would help. By the time she got to deck 1, she saw Admiral Esrith walk into the lounge ahead of her.

Damn! She wanted to drink alone. Esrith liked to talk. She moved to the bar on the side away from the admiral.

"Hello, Captain!" Lieutenant Eno ni Esrith said. Eno was taller than his 6'5" admiral father, but with his white-blond hair and pale blue eyes, was otherwise the spitting image of his Chromian parent. Both men were pleasant to look at, but could be very intimidating when they wanted to be.

"Lieutenant," she nodded. "I'll have a Detonator," she said to the barkeep. It was the strongest drink she could tolerate.

"Something must be going on to have three officers in here this early," Lieutenant Eno said as he sipped his drink.

"Something indeed," Admiral Esrith said, moving toward them.

"I'll say," the barkeep added. "This is the fifth Detonator I've made in the last ten minutes.

Gadara glanced at the two Esrith men and the barkeep. "Who are the other two for?"

Before he could answer, the door hissed open and two people stepped inside.

"Lieutenant Tremol and Keely." Admiral Esrith raised his glass to them. "I believe you know Lieutenant Tremol, Captain Gadara?"

"Lieutenant Tremol of the Interplanetary Space Patrol?" she asked. Tremol was definitely Caucus with his dark hair and brown eyes, but he had two inches on her six-foot frame. She'd seen him on the ship before arriving in Earth's atmosphere.

"Yes, and this is his mate, Keely ni Tremol, a Secret Service Agent from the Earthen Delegation. They recently met on Earth and I performed the ceremony here on the Concordance."

Keely was definitely new. She would have remembered someone like her with all that dark orange hair, blue eyes, and all those little brown dots across her face.

"She looks like the Huanti from Plexus," Gadara said.

"That's what Tremol told me when we first met," Keely

said. "I know this was a short engagement period. We barely know each other, but I feel as if we get along well, we're both in law enforcement, and we have a lifetime to get to know each other." She glanced at Tremol and smiled.

"They are the first liaisons for the new Delegations between Earth and Vaedra," Lieutenant Eno added.

The barkeep slid two Detonators toward Tremol and one toward Gadara.

Tremol reached for the two drinks and handed one to Keely. Gadara picked up her Detonator.

"May we get to our destination unencumbered." The admiral toasted them.

The five officers lifted their glasses and sipped their drinks when the door to the Officers Lounge hissed open.

My own mix just for the story

The Concordance (Deposit Photos)

Landing Bay inside the Concordance (Deposit Photos)

8

EXCERPT FROM BATTLE FOR EARTH

Chapter One

The White House

"Mr. President, I'm Chief Medical Officer Conn from the Concordance, and these are my counterparts, CMO Shim from the Reliance and CMO Torres from the Endeavor." She shook the outstretched hand of the President, and watched as the others did the same.

"We are also healers," she said.

"Have a seat," the President said. He gestured to the chairs in the room.

She bowed and sat down. "The three of us have been working in our labs, creating the blood test that will show you who is human and who is not."

"We have blood tests here as well," the President said.

"Yes, but I assure you, this test will let you know immediately so you can take swift action."

"What do you mean by that?"

"The Draconians won't stand still for this. They will fight

or run. If they refuse the test, we have our security forces who will stun them temporarily so they can be tested. If they are not human, you must decide whether to destroy them or hold them prisoners."

"Do you think it's that serious?" the President asked.

"Yes, sir. It is," CMO Torres said. "The Draconians embed themselves into government agencies where they take over that government."

"They gain control of planets from within," Conn said.

"Have you had recent turmoil and violence in your part of your world?" CMO Shim asked.

"Yes, actually. It's been happening all over the planet, especially after UFO sightings," the President said.

"UFO sightings?" Conn asked.

"Unidentified flying objects," the President said.

"It is worse than I thought," Conn said. She glanced at her counterparts.

"Do you have labs that can duplicate our blood tests?" CMO Torres asked.

"Yes, we do."

"We need to test everyone at the lab first to avoid sabotage. We also need to test everyone in your government," Conn said.

"Everyone?"

"Yes, sir. Otherwise, you won't know whom to trust," CMO Torres said.

The Concordance, Above Earth's Moon

Adam Davis paced back and forth in the small quarters he shared with his mate. "Genesis, I can't stand by and do nothing." He ran a hand through his hair. "That's my planet. My home."

"And my home is with you," she said. She stood and touched his arm.

He stopped pacing.

"Whatever you decide, I am with you."

"Let's go find Tremol and see what we can do," he said. He put his arm around her and headed to the people mover.

Captain Tremol and his mate, Keely, sat across from Captain Gadara and her mate, Torren Conley, in the Officers Lounge on deck 1.

Keely waved them over. Adam sat next to Torren and Genesis sat next to Keely.

"When do you start your new assignment?" Keely asked Captain Gadara.

"We start tomorrow," she said. She touched Torren's thigh and squeezed.

He smiled at her before speaking. "They are sending us to Edwards Air Force Base." He glanced at Keely and Captain Tremol.

"Edwards? Isn't that where they keep alien ships?" Keely asked.

"Yes. We will be training for two months before they send us to the moons of Mars," Gadara said. She smiled at Torren. He winked at her.

"What about you two?" Keely glanced at him and Genesis.

"That's why we are here," Genesis said.

The barkeep brought some drinks for Tremol, Keely, Gadara, and Torren. "What are you two having?"

"Two ales, please," Adam said.

When the barkeep left, Adam glanced at Tremol. "What's the word on Earth?"

"Conn and the Chief Medical Officers from the Reliance and Endeavor left with their assistants and security for the White House," Tremol said.

"They are initiating the testing," Keely added. "We were told to wait here for further instructions."

"What about all the dignitaries?" Adam asked.

"After they were all tested here, Keely and I flew them to the White House with our security. They are in a bunker, on lockdown, until the building is cleared of all Draconians," Tremol said.

"Genesis and I want to help. What can we do?" he asked.

The barkeep returned with his drinks. Before leaving, he glanced at the entrance. Everyone turned to see Admiral Esrith walk in with Eno and a couple other people.

"We just got word from the Reliance that their scientists have created a mist that will penetrate the skin of non-humans and expose who they really are. It's much quicker than the blood tests." The admiral, Eno, and the two others stood beside their table.

"Something tells me there's bad news with this," Adam said.

"You're right, Adam. The word from the Endeavor is the damn reptiles have taken over the White House."

The Reliance from the Vaedra System (Deposit Photos)

The Endeavor from the Vaedra System (Deposit Photos)

Wing ship from the Concordance (Deposit Photos)

Cockpit of the Wing ships (Deposit Photos)

Wedge ship from Concordance (Deposit Photos)

Concordance Cargo Transport Leaving Chroma (Deposit Photos)

THE VAEDRA CHRONICLES SERIES BOOK 5
BATTLE
FOR EARTH
ESTER LÓPEZ

9

UNIFORMS (UNICRINS) OF THE VAEDRAN MILITARY

*Land Force Insignia for Vaedran Planetary Military - Unicrins
(uniforms) are green and they cover land, sea, and air*

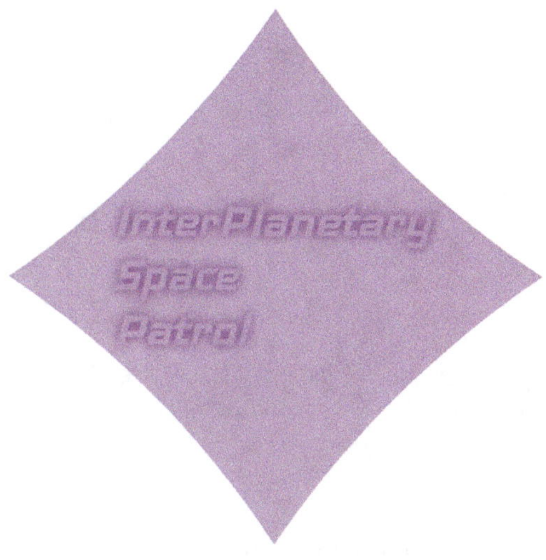

ISP Insignia for Vaedran Paramilitary Law Enforcement between the planets - Unicrins are white

Unicrins of the ISP and weapons (Deposit Photos)

Star Force Insignia for Vaedran Military in Space - Unicrins are black for pilots, gray for technicians, white for officers

SHIPS OF THE INTERPLANETARY SPACE PATROL

ISP Wing Ship 1 (Pixaby)

ISP Wing Ship 2 (Deposit Photos)

ISP Wedge Ships (Deposit Photos)

ISP Cargo Transport (Deposit Photos)

ISP Guardian Class (Deposit Photos)

11

SPACE STATIONS AND INDIE SPACE PORTS

ISP Space Ports - 4 Total - located throughout the Vaedra System
(Deposit Photos)

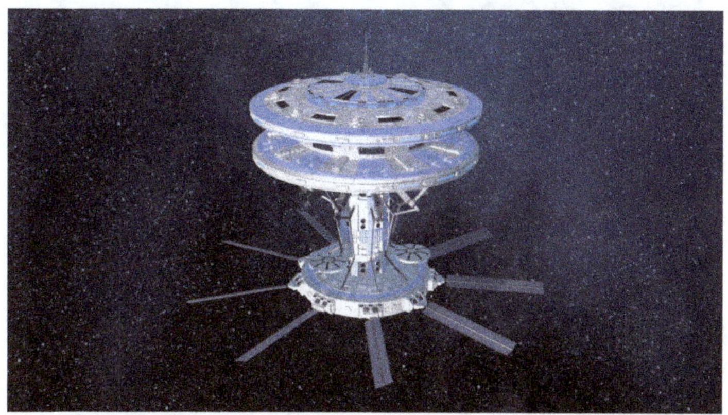

Independent Space Stations, monitored by the ISP (Deposit Photos)

On the Quinna Space Port, hovering over Tewa, Tarsius, we find the Stellar Voyager Eatery & Lounge. The Lounge sits on the lower tier of the Quinna Space Port and run by Mariposa, Berto's sister.

12

WEAPONS OF THE VAEDRAN MILITARY

*This weapon was taken from the Greys and Reptilians -
it can melt things or disintegrate things (Deposit Photos)
in Battle for Earth*

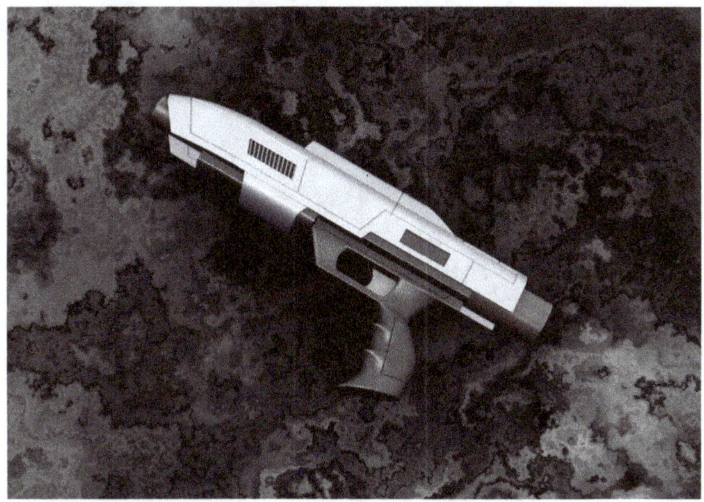

This weapon is a stunner and can also kill (Deposit Photos) in The Abduction

This is an Ion Cannon used in The Abduction (Deposit Photos)

13

———————

VIEWS FROM THE PLANETS

View of Vestra Minor from the ocean (Deposit Photos)

Another Interior View of Vestra Minor (Deposit Photos)

City view of Persus (Deposit Photos)

Country view of Persus (Deposit Photos)

Vestra Major along the ocean (Deposit Photos)

Interior of Atria (Deposit Photos)

Atria overlooking it's moon, Adara (Deposit Photos)

Plumaris, overlooking it's moon, Ata (Deposit Photos)

Meta, a moon of Plexus, overlooking Plexus and Tiga (Deposit Photos)

Chroma, overlooking one of it's moons, Creton (Deposit Photos)

City view of Plexus, overlooking it's moon, Nela, from a people mover (Deposit Photos)

14

EXCERPT FROM REDEMPTION

BOOK ONE IN THE VAEDRA SAGA

Dram aimed the AI powered plasma drill at the target and squeezed the handles. In a matter of minutes, liquid tulin poured into the wheeled vat below the hole. When it reached the fill line, he had the next vat lined up.

"Vat's up!" he yelled. He pushed the full vat down the track and concentrated on filling the new vat.

Gomet grabbed the vat and pushed it to the next link, where the tulin would be poured into the grand vat. From there, it would be made into coins or bars or melted into exquisite furniture.

He remembered when he owned furniture made of tulin and spent the coins on ships to increase his business.

He lined up the plasma drill once more when the flow of tulin stopped. Pressing the handles, he tried to get more tulin to pour out, but this vein was done. He reached up and pulled the sensor down to locate more of the shiny gold-colored metal.

Moving the sensor around, up and down the rock wall, it

finally beeped. He marked the spot and moved his vat into place and began the same routine. More liquid tulin flowed after the plasma drill did its thing.

He couldn't imagine doing this kind of work without these tools. The only reason humans were needed was to move the vats along and to manually use the sensor. Oh, and the fact that it was punishment for living a life of crime. Yeah, that's the reason.

"I heard we were getting another cell-mate," Gomet said.

"Did you, now?" He pushed the filled vat to Gomet.

He walked back a ways to pick up another empty vat and push it along to his target area. He could only get so much out of a vein with one blast.

"So, when is this new cell-mate coming in?" he asked. He aimed his plasma drill again and blasted another vein of tulin.

He watched the liquid pour into the vat.

"Tonight," Gomet said.

"Hmmm." Gomet usually got good intel. A new cellmate didn't come along too often. It would be amusing for a while, but then he would get bored harassing the newbie. But cellmates didn't mean they would be working together. They would just be sleeping in the same cell. Right now, it was him, Gomet, and Thadus. After this newbie, there were no more beds.

Thadus worked the gem mines. The work was harder, but not as hot. Here, in the tulin mines, the high heat to melt the tulin into coins, bars, or furnishings kept the whole place sweltering. His tank top was grimy and worn and so were his pants. Once every six months, they were given some clean, recycled clothes and the old ones were washed and passed along to someone else.

Thadus used his chisel to work the rubies out of their rock enclosure. He had an eye for detail, and this was slow, tedious work. The more he was able to pry the bigger rubies out, the bigger his bonus at the end of the month.

He hung from his harness over a wall of sparkling rubies. Besides himself, there were two others who could dislodge the beauties in big pieces. They all wanted that bonus. He was planning on buying a pillow with his earnings. The flattened pillow he had was giving him neck pains and he dreamed of a good night's sleep.

Once a month, when the bonuses were given out, they had a small market set up where the prisoners could buy things they needed or wanted, luxury items that normal people took for granted.

"Thadus!"

He turned to see who called him. That was odd because no one ever called him. He caught a glimpse of movement below him on a ledge.

"Coming up!" a voice called out.

Within seconds, a woman was hoisted up next to him in a harness. Her hair was black with orange spikes coming out from it, reminding him of a matchstick.

"I'm Tam," she said.

"Well, I'm Thadus. I guess you're the newbie I heard talk about."

"I guess so."

"Let me show you what I'm doing and then you can attack that wall over there."

He reached above her head and pulled her rope closer to his. He showed her how to hold the chisel and the mallet, then went to work.

"It's simple really. If you take your time and do it right, you get a bonus each month for the big rubies. If you break them, you get nothing."

"I didn't think prisoners got paid at all," she said.

"We don't. The bonus helps to buy things like a blanket or pillow or clothes. Just a little something to make our hell on Plumaris a little easier to bear."

Thadus reached up to the rope above her harness, and shoved

Tam further away.

"That's the end of your lesson. You're on your own now."

"Thanks," she mumbled.

Thadus went back to work. Each ruby he extracted was carefully placed into a bag he had on his waist.

"Where's my bag?" Tam asked.

"Didn't they give you one?"

"Nope."

Thadus patted his grimy clothes and found a spare bag. He pushed off from the rock wall and slid sideways to reach Tam.

"Here. You should have gotten one when they hooked you up to the harness."

"I guess they overlooked that part," she said.

Hours later, an alarm sounded, and the harnesses were lowered to the ground.

"What's happening?" Tam asked.

"It's quitting time," Thadus said.

A guard unhooked each of them from their harness and pointed to a wall with a box protruding out from it.

"Deposit your rubies with your code over there," the guard said.

"What code?" Tam asked.

"Weren't you given a code when they processed you?"

"I don't remember a code."

"Name?"

"Tam."

"Your code is 043," the guard said. He glanced at his comm-pad. "Don't forget that number. You need it for everything."

"Yes, sir." Tam walked to the box and pressed her code into the keypad beside it and it opened. She deposited her rubies inside the box and the box closed.

"Now what?" she said.

"You go to your cell," the guard said.

"She's a newbie," Thadus said. "I don't think she has been assigned a cell yet."

"Wait there," the guard said. He pointed to a spot against the wall.

After Thadus and two others deposited their rubies and went on, the guard approached her.

"Come with me," he said.

"Is this our daily routine, then?" Tam asked.

"You came late today. Tomorrow, you eat breakfast and put in ten hours with two breaks and a lunch then go back to your cell at the end of the day."

"Sounds like fun." Tam said, sarcastically.

The guard gave her a side glance.

They walked through the tunnel before getting into a people
    mover. After a few minutes, the people mover stopped, and they
    exited.

"This is your cell block." The guard checked his comm-pad again. "This way." He turned right and she followed him down a hall. It looked more like a building than a cave. Each cell appeared to have four men in them. There were cells on each side of the hall. The guard stopped at the last one on the right and unlocked the cell.

There was Thadus, along with two others.

"There must be some mistake," she said.

"No. This is your cell."

"Where are the women's cells?"

"You're the first, so there aren't any," the guard said.

All three men stood frozen, glancing at each other, then her, then the guard.

"You've got to be kidding," a tall Chromian said.

"Enjoy the company, boys." The guard shoved her inside and closed the cell.

"Hello, Tam," Thadus said.

Now that she could actually see, she realized he was Caucasian and so was the other man. All three were a bit grimy and...old.

Her stomach growled, reminding her she hadn't eaten all day. She hoped there was a meal tonight.

"There's your bed," the Chromian said. He pointed to the

bunk on top. It had a mattress, but that was all. No sheets, no pillow.

"Thanks," she said. She climbed up the side to get to her bunk. She was tired. But then, she remembered she had to pee. She climbed back down.

"Where's the toilet?"

All three men stepped aside, and she could see it, out in the open, with a sink beside it.

Great. No privacy. And no shower. Well, she had to go and there wasn't anything she could do about it. She just pretended they weren't there and did her business. Maybe it would get easier. But when she finished, she realized, they had all turned their backs to her. Hmm. Is this what they did for each other, too?

Before she could climb up to the top bunk, the Chromian grabbed her arm.

"What are you doing here? You're just a kid."

"I'm older than I look, old man."

"Old man?" Thadus asked.

The other Caucasian laughed.

"I asked you a question," the Chromian said.

She glanced at his hand, still holding her arm, then glared into his eyes.

"I poisoned a man, sabotaged a couple ships, and tried to

kill another man, is that okay with you?"

"Did you say you sabotaged a couple ships?" Thadus asked.

"That's right." The Chromian pulled her toward him as the other two gathered around.

"I remember you. You're the one that helped us find that traitor, Berto."

"Yes. You were with the pirates that boarded the ship we were on."

"Berto? The man with telekinetic powers?" The Chromian asked.

"That's the one," she said.

"How do you know Berto?" Thadus asked the Chromian.

"He worked for me," the Chromian said.

"Well, it looks like we all have something in common, don't we?" She said.

The Chromian turned her loose. She looked him over. For an old man, he had a nice body, which was more than she could say for the other two.

"How do you know Berto?" The Chromian asked her.

"He killed my brother."

www.ingramcontent.com/pod-product-compliance
Lightning Source LLC
Chambersburg PA
CBHW071200300726

48975CB00004B/1227